"I had planned on an e̶a̶r̶l̶y̶ ̶n̶i̶g̶h̶t̶,̶ ̶b̶u̶t̶ ̶c̶o̶u̶l̶d̶n̶'̶t̶ ̶p̶u̶t̶ ̶i̶t̶ ̶d̶own until I finished it around 3am. L̶i̶k̶e̶ ̶h̶e̶r̶ ̶other books, this one features fascinating characters with a plot that mimics real life in the best way. My recommendation: it's time to read every book Tammy L Grace has written."
— *Carolyn, review of Beach Haven*

"This book is a clean, simple romance with a background story very similar to the works of Debbie Macomber. If you like Macomber's books you will like this one. A holiday tale filled with dogs, holiday fun, and the joy of giving will warm your heart."
— *Avid Mystery Reader, review of A Season for Hope: A Christmas Novella*

"This book was just as enchanting as the others. Hardships with the love of a special group of friends. I recommend the series as a must read. I loved every exciting moment. A new author for me. She's fabulous."
—*Maggie!, review of Pieces of Home: A Hometown Harbor Novel (Book 4)*

"Tammy is an amazing author, she reminds me of Debbie Macomber… Delightful, heartwarming…just down to earth."
— *Plee, review of A Promise of Home: A Hometown Harbor Novel (Book 3)*

"This was an entertaining and relaxing novel. Tammy Grace has a simple yet compelling way of drawing the reader into the lives of her characters. It was a pleasure to read a story that didn't rely on theatrical tricks, unrealistic events or steamy sex scenes to fill up the pages. Her characters and plot were strong enough to hold the reader's interest."
—*MrsQ125, review of Finding Home: A Hometown Harbor Novel (Book 1)*

"This is a beautifully written story of loss, grief, forgiveness and healing. I believe anyone could relate to the situations and feelings represented here. This is a read that will stay with you long after you've completed the book."
—*Cassidy Hop, review of Finally Home: A Hometown Harbor Novel (Book 5)*

"Killer Music is a clever and well-crafted whodunit. The vivid and colorful characters shine as the author gradually reveals their hidden secrets—an absorbing page-turning read."

— *Jason Deas, bestselling author of Pushed and Birdsongs*

"I could not put this book down! It was so well written & a suspenseful read! This is definitely a 5-star story! I'm hoping there will be a sequel!"
—*Colleen, review of Killer Music*

"This is the best book yet by this author. The plot was well crafted with an unanticipated ending. I like to try to leap ahead and see if I can accurately guess the outcome. I was able to predict some of the plot but not the actual details which made reading the last several chapters quite engrossing."
—*0001PW, review of Deadly Connection*

GREETINGS FROM LAVENDER VALLEY

SISTERS OF THE HEART BOOK 1

TAMMY L. GRACE

LONE MOUNTAIN PRESS

Greetings from Lavender Valley
Sisters of the Heart Series
Tammy L. Grace

GREETINGS FROM LAVENDER VALLEY is a work of fiction. Names, characters, places, and incidents either are products of the author's imagination or are used fictitiously. Any resemblance to actual events, locales, entities, or persons, living or dead, is entirely coincidental.

GREETINGS FROM LAVENDER VALLEY Copyright © 2023 by Tammy L. Grace

All rights reserved. No part of this book may be reproduced or transmitted in any form or by any means, electronic or mechanical including photocopying, recording, or by any information storage and retrieval system without the written permission of the author, except for the use of brief quotations in a book review. For permissions contact the author directly via electronic mail: tammy@tammylgrace.com

www.tammylgrace.com
Facebook: https://www.facebook.com/tammylgrace.books
Twitter: @TammyLGrace
Instagram: @authortammylgrace
Published in the United States by Lone Mountain Press, Nevada

ISBN (eBook) 978-1-945591-41-9
ISBN (Print) 978-1-945591-51-8
FIRST EDITION
Printed in the United States of America
Cover Design by Elizabeth Mackey Graphic Design

ALSO BY TAMMY L. GRACE

COOPER HARRINGTON DETECTIVE NOVELS
Killer Music
Deadly Connection
Dead Wrong
Cold Killer

HOMETOWN HARBOR SERIES
Hometown Harbor: The Beginning (Prequel Novella)
Finding Home
Home Blooms
A Promise of Home
Pieces of Home
Finally Home
Forever Home
Follow Me Home

CHRISTMAS STORIES
A Season for Hope: Christmas in Silver Falls Book 1
The Magic of the Season: Christmas in Silver Falls Book 2
Christmas in Snow Valley: A Hometown Christmas Book 1
One Unforgettable Christmas: A Hometown Christmas Book 2
Christmas Wishes: Souls Sisters at Cedar Mountain Lodge
Christmas Surprises: Soul Sisters at Cedar Mountain Lodge

GLASS BEACH COTTAGE SERIES

Beach Haven

Moonlight Beach

Beach Dreams

WRITING AS CASEY WILSON

A Dog's Hope

A Dog's Chance

WISHING TREE SERIES

The Wishing Tree

Wish Again

Overdue Wishes

SISTERS OF THE HEART SERIES

Greetings from Lavender Valley

Pathway to Lavender Valley

Sanctuary at Lavender Valley

Remember to subscribe to Tammy's exclusive group of readers for your gift, only available to readers on her mailing list. **Sign up at www.tammylgrace.com.** Follow this link to subscribe at https://**wp.me/P9umIy-e** and you'll receive the exclusive interview she did with all the canine characters in her Hometown Harbor Series.

Follow Tammy on Facebook by liking her page. You may also follow Tammy on book retailers or at BookBub by clicking on the follow button.

For foster parents everywhere

JEWEL

THE ARRIVAL

Jewel swept her eyes over the upstairs bedroom one more time. She ran her hand over the gingham bedspread and straightened the matching pillow sham, then moved to the white bookcase she had painted herself and touched the spines of the *Little House on the Prairie* books, adjusting one of them that was sticking out from the others. Shelved beside them, the *Anne of Green Gables* series she had found at a yard sale looked like new. She couldn't wait to share the books with the girl who would soon be sleeping in the sunlit room.

Jewel adjusted the vase on the bedside table and bent to sniff the fresh lilacs she had trimmed from the bushes along the fence. The delightful smell infused the air, reminding Jewel of her grandmother.

This wasn't her first trip up the stairs to check on the room she had spent hours preparing, but it was almost three o'clock and she had to take one last look. She couldn't resist one more adjustment to the eyelet valance above the window before she dashed downstairs.

The social worker from Medford was due in a few

minutes and Jewel wanted everything perfect. She ran the cloth over the counter in the kitchen before she put the kettle on to boil and straightened the napkins on the tea tray.

Jewel had spent last night making three kinds of cookies to have on hand for the young girl she would soon meet. Georgia was her name. Such a grown-up name for a little girl of twelve.

The farmhouse was spotless, with every window gleaming in the spring sunshine bathing Lavender Valley Farm. Jewel's nerves were getting the best of her as she paced the floor. The sound of the kettle beckoned her back to the stove and with shaking fingers, she held the lid of the kettle and poured the boiling water into her teapot.

As she did so, she gasped. No twelve-year-old girl was going to want a cup of tea. What was she thinking? She replaced the hot kettle on the burner and hurried to the freezer. She popped open a can of frozen lemonade concentrate and spooned it into a pitcher.

A bead of sweat formed at the base of Jewel's neck as she rushed to stir the lemonade with a wooden spoon. She added some ice cubes, wiped the counter again, and placed the pitcher on the dining room table, along with the tea service.

She sighed as she put her hands on her hips. "There, that's better."

Beau, her golden retriever, sauntered to the door, his tail wagging in quick arcs. He was her early alert system. Jewel took off her apron, straightened her skirt, and made sure her crisp blouse was tucked in before following Beau to the front door.

He was a sweet and friendly dog, but Jewel wasn't sure how Georgia would react to him. She shooed him over to his fluffy bed in the living room and told him to stay there.

Jewel took a deep breath and counted to ten before opening the front door, then hurried across the porch to greet her guests. Mrs. Parsons, the social worker, who had a permanent scowl etched on her wide face, walked up the porch steps, holding the hand of a tall, slim girl with long reddish-brown braids, as if making sure she wouldn't escape. The young girl, wearing a print dress with a frayed hem, carried a battered suitcase, and Mrs. Parsons gripped the handles of a worn, fabric bag.

Jewel caught the girl's eye. The poor thing look terrified, her brown eyes wide and her face pale. She reminded Jewel of a wary doe. "Hello, Georgia. I'm Jewel. May I take that bag for you?" She extended her hand.

Georgia nodded but said nothing, even as Jewel took the bag from her.

Jewel held the front door open for both of them. "I've got some refreshments made for us, but I can show you your bedroom first. It's just up the stairs."

Georgia remained silent.

Jewel looked to Mrs. Parsons for guidance, but didn't get as much as a nod from her. Jewel gripped the suitcase tighter and led the way up the stairs.

She gestured at the open door. "This is it. I can help you get your things organized and put away later." She pointed at the small white desk that matched the bookcase. "My husband, Chuck, made that desk for you, so you'd have a spot to do your homework. You'll meet him tonight."

Jewel set the suitcase down next to the dresser and took the tote bag from Mrs. Parsons. She put the bag in the chair in the corner, where a stuffed bear rested. "I wasn't sure if you were too old for stuffed animals," she said to Georgia, trying again. "But when I saw this guy, I thought he'd be a perfect roommate for you."

Without a word, Georgia moved toward the bear and brushed her hand over its head.

Mrs. Parsons studied the room and rewarded Jewel with a curt nod. In profile, Jewel realized what a pointy nose the woman had and thought she'd make the perfect witch for Halloween. She shoved that thought away, lest she giggle.

Jewel felt like she was back in high school, awaiting judgment from the English teacher nobody liked. Her heart broke for Georgia, who looked as terrified as Jewel had felt back then. "How about we have some cookies? I've got them waiting in the dining room."

Mrs. Parsons led the way down the stairs, followed by Georgia. Jewel noticed the slump in the girl's shoulders as she trudged down each step.

Jewel poured lemonade for Georgia first. With a smile, Jewel set the glass in front of her and offered her first choice from the plate of cookies. "I've got chocolate chip, snickerdoodle, and peanut butter."

Georgia took a snickerdoodle, and Mrs. Parsons waved the plate away.

With her stomach fluttering, Jewel was certain she must have swallowed one of the butterflies that flew around the lilacs as she poured tea for Mrs. Parsons and herself. Then she took a cookie and added it to her plate, with the hope a nibble would give her stomach something productive to do.

Mrs. Parsons took a file from her handbag, and before Jewel could swallow a sip from her cup, started bombarding her with information related to the middle school Georgia would attend in Medford, the bus schedule, the home visits Mrs. Parsons would be performing to check on Jewel and Chuck, and a stack of forms related to medical care and reimbursement paperwork.

With her spiel delivered, Mrs. Parsons took one gulp

from her cup and stood. "Well, I'll be going. I'll check on you in two weeks, Mrs. Austin, unless you need something before then." She narrowed her eyes at Georgia. "You be a good young lady."

Jewel swallowed the lump in her throat and hurried to get out of her chair. By the time she reached the front door, Mrs. Parsons was already down the steps and heading to her old county issued station wagon.

The driver's door slammed shut and the engine roared to life.

Jewel stood on her porch, and with an immense sigh of relief, watched the car head down their long driveway. Mrs. Parsons terrified her. She could only imagine the impact she had on children.

Back inside, Beau raised his head to look at her hopefully. Jewel held up her hand. "Just a minute, boy."

She went into the kitchen and sat down next to Georgia again. "That woman scares me," she said, before taking a bite of her cookie. She stole a glance at the young girl, but Georgia didn't react at all.

The social worker had only told Jewel and Chuck that Georgia's mother was deceased and her father in prison. There were no relatives that would take her in. She had a younger sister, who was not quite two years old and had already been placed with a family in Portland who wanted to adopt her.

When they'd asked about the prospect of someone adopting Georgia, Mrs. Parsons laughed. She told them they were naïve and didn't understand that nobody wanted to adopt the older kids.

The blank and sad look on Georgia's face was enough to bring tears to Jewel's eyes. She blinked several times as she hid her mouth behind her teacup. She had to get through to the poor girl sitting at her table. Chuck had voiced his concern that Jewel's heart might be too soft to take on fostering. Still reeling with the news from the doctor that they could never have children, he didn't want more sadness inflicted upon his wife.

"Chuck will be home from his job at the road department in an hour or so. He's looking forward to meeting you. I've got a meatloaf ready to put in the oven. Do you like meatloaf? I'm making some potatoes and green beans to go with it."

Georgia nodded. "Yes, ma'am."

"You can call me Jewel, sweetie." She glanced across to the living room. "I want to introduce you to my very best friend. Do you like dogs?"

Georgia nodded and used her napkin to wipe her hands.

Jewel whistled and Beau came charging around the corner, tail wagging, tongue out. He bypassed Jewel and went right to Georgia, wiggling as he placed his head in her lap, then started to lift his paws. Worried he might be too much for her, Jewel jumped from her chair, scraping it across the wooden floor.

Georgia flinched and shrunk away, her gaze focused on the ground. With slower movements, Jewel stepped to the other side of Georgia's chair and put gentle hands on Beau's shoulders to help him remember to keep his paws on the floor. What she ached to do instead was to wrap the poor girl in a hug. She could only imagine what Georgia had been through in her short life. Part of her didn't want to know.

Now, more than ever, she wanted to earn Georgia's trust and comfort her. Without much experience with children, she wasn't sure how to accomplish it, but Jewel had good instincts and trusted her heart to guide her.

Her heart warmed as Georgia's hand moved from her lap

to the top of Beau's head. He stretched his big tongue out and gave her a quick lick.

Not quite a smile, but the edges of Georgia's lips lifted ever so slightly and her eyes softened when they found Beau's.

That tiny sparkle of encouragement was all Jewel needed. She would find a way to connect with Georgia and would give her all the love she already held in her heart. She might not have a child related to her, but she would make a difference in Georgia's life, and in the lives of as many children like her that Jackson County saw fit to place in her care.

GEORGIA

APRIL 1974

JEWEL'S JOURNAL

Oh, Georgia. Tonight's your first night staying here on the farm with us. I've been a nervous wreck all day and wanted so much to make a good impression on you.

I had hoped Mrs. Parsons would grow on me, but after having her at the house, I'm not sure she's capable of much kindness. I'm sure she's dutiful about her job, but she sure lacks the compassion I would suspect someone in her position to possess.

I know you're not from Lavender Valley, or even Medford, so I know a new home and a new school will be a big adjustment. When I asked Mrs. Parsons if there was anything special you liked, she mentioned books and reading. I enjoy reading too, and can't wait to introduce you to the characters in the books I stocked in your room.

As soon as you want, I'll take you to the library and get you a library card. We'll have such fun visiting and finding new books to read.

I worry that you're so quiet, and while I was trying not to watch over you and make you nervous, I couldn't help but notice you didn't eat your cookie this afternoon. I understand, believe me. Mrs. Parsons almost made me too nervous to eat.

Instead, I saw you slip it into the pocket of your dress and when I was taking the dishes to the sink, I saw you take another one and put it in your other pocket.

I pretended not to notice. I also pretended not to see the old bruises on your upper arms and across your back when I helped you get ready for bed tonight.

I'm not sure what happened to you, but I know whatever it was, it won't happen here. Chuck and I will never hurt you and we'll do all we can to help you heal and build a life here on the farm.

I hope I can convince you to trust me and to talk to me. The only bit of emotion I saw came when Beau put his head in your lap and later tonight when he slipped into your bedroom and sat next to you. He's concerned about you, and I hope he's giving you a bit of courage. He's done that for me on more than one occasion. We all need a reminder that we're strong and brave.

I know you are, dear girl.

I cannot wait to get to know you and help you heal.

JANUARY 1975

JEWEL'S JOURNAL

What progress we've made in the last year, Georgia. One of my favorite memories was of your first Christmas with us, when you unwrapped that sewing machine. I felt bad that it wasn't brand new, but I don't think you cared one bit. It hasn't stopped humming since Chuck set it up for you in the cottage.

I like thinking of the cottage as our secret clubhouse. We've got the sewing room and the planting room, where I can keep all my seed and bulb catalogs and can start them growing indoors. Chuck still has work to do on it and the other cottage, not to mention the barn, but it's fun to have our own space for our hobbies.

He's such a good man and I'm lucky to have him. He always supports whatever goofy idea I come up with. I have one brewing right now and am waiting for the right time to spring it on him.

As I write this, I'm admiring the new apron you made me. It's perfect with all the pockets for my planting tools. I'm even more excited that the library is offering a crochet and knitting class, and that you signed up. You are so talented with a needle, I have no doubt you'll quickly master both of them.

Mostly, I'm happy you're smiling more. You're still awfully quiet, but I've come to understand you're a thinker. You do much more thinking than talking. I know a few people that should do the same. I do enjoy our chats when you tell me about the latest book you're reading. I must say, *Les Miserables* is quite the feat for a girl in eighth grade.

We're so proud of you and are happy you're part of our family.

MARCH 1977

JEWEL'S JOURNAL

Georgia, you are blossoming before my eyes. Your talent and generosity is so wonderful to see unfold. Ever since Dale and Suzannah arrived, months ago now, you've been the perfect big sister.

You talk to little Dale about his love of the horses and tell him he's so strong when he helps around the farm. It's like you understand that he needs someone to believe in him.

Then, when Suzannah's doll's dress got so filthy and she refused to let me wash it, you, my sweet hearted girl, took it upon yourself to make a new set of dresses for Dolly. They're made from scraps, but they're beautiful. You even added little touches like buttons and lace collars. I am amazed by your patience and talent! Miss Suzannah lit up like a Christmas bulb when she untied the ribbon on the gift and peeked inside.

And today. Oh my! I had a hard time not blubbering when Suzannah even let you mend a few seams on Dolly's arms and legs. Then the idea to have a Dolly fashion show, with cookies afterward. It was a wonderful day that I will always treasure.

JUNE 1979

JEWEL'S JOURNAL

Oh, Georgia, my grown-up girl. Watching you graduate today was the highlight of my year. Chuck had to loan me his handkerchief because mine was sopping wet from tears by the time you walked across the stage.

The blue dress you made is gorgeous and looks fancier than all the store-bought ones I saw. I'm so proud of you being in Honor Society and wearing that special sash over your gown.

I will treasure the photo you took with Chuck and me outside the school. You look so happy. I know you're nervous about going to Eastern Oregon University, but I have faith in you, my dear. You earned that scholarship because you are smart and talented. You may not be sure of exactly what you want to do yet, but I think your choice in getting a teaching degree is a good one. You can always change your mind if you find out it's not for you. It will give you lots of options in the future, no matter what you decide.

I know how much you enjoy reading and spending your time studying, but I hope you remember to reach out and meet people too. Le Grande is a beautiful small town and I know you'll love it there.

I will miss you so much. I didn't know what I was doing when you first arrived. Thank goodness, you were patient, and we learned together. I'll always be grateful to you for helping heal my heart. You were the first young girl who trusted me, and in doing so, helped open the door for others.

JUNE 20, 1985

Dear Georgia,

Congratulations on your marriage! I wish we could have gotten away to attend the wedding, but the farm never takes a day off and we have four children in our care who need us. I do hope you know how very happy we are for you.

You deserve a lifetime of joy and I'm thrilled you found such a good man as Lee. I remember the excitement of starting married life together with Chuck. It's such a wonderful time of new experiences.

With shopping limited in Lavender Valley, it's hard to find a suitable wedding gift to ship, so I've included some money and I hope you and Lee will use it for something you want, or splurge and go to a fancy dinner somewhere.

I'm glad Lee found a teaching position, and although I haven't been to the Boise area in years, I remember it being quite beautiful. I think you'll enjoy it, but be prepared for snow in the winter.

I know you're disappointed that you haven't finished

college and graduated yet, but you have your whole life in front of you. Above all, you need to be happy and enjoy your life. You can always go back to school in Boise and finish up the last few classes.

I still can't believe that shy, young girl, our first child, is married. I'm starting to feel old!

If you ever get back this way, do stop in and say hello. We'd love to have you visit.

Wishing you many years of blessings and happiness, along with a bit of adventure.

Love from,
Jewel and Chuck

JANUARY 2, 2003

Dear Georgia,

Thank you for the lovely holiday card and the beautiful scarf you knitted. I'm glad to hear you're working at the school library and enjoying it. You always had a love for books. Sometimes I worried about you huddled in a chair with your nose in a book, but I soon figured out that that was your happy place. You lived through the pages of those stories and they let you escape.

Not only is working in the library a perfect fit for you, but working at the school will allow you and Lee to share all the same time off together. It gives you some freedom in the summer to travel or do whatever you want.

I wrapped your scarf around my neck first thing this morning, and it's so soft and luxurious. I'm almost afraid to wear it, especially around the dogs. They'll be attracted to the fringe. I think I'll save it for church.

I'm thrilled to know you kept up on your sewing and knitting skills. You had such a natural talent and could make anything. I remember you spending your spare time sewing doll clothes so you could surprise the younger girls at Christmas. Talk about patience! I can patch a shirt or hem a pair of pants, even knit or crotchet a simple blanket, but designing clothes, especially for dolls, is something I could never accomplish.

I so enjoyed it when you and Lee visited a few years ago. I hope you'll plan another trip soon and stay with us. We'd love to see you.

Happy New Year with love,
   Jewel and Chuck

MAY 3, 2008

Dear Georgia,

I'm writing to share the sad news that Chuck passed away last month. I intended to write earlier, but just ran out of steam. I am heartbroken, but at the same time thankful for the almost fifty years we shared as a couple. He was the best man I ever knew, and I miss him fiercely.

I'm still exhausted from trying to keep up with the farm and tending to Chuck, but did a good job of hiding it from him. I hated to worry him. Now, however, I'm at the point I have to find some help. There's too much to do and not enough hours in the day.

I've got a call in to a few people in town to see if I can find a farmhand and will be offering a very small salary, along with room and board in the bunkhouse. Chuck and I talked about that idea before he got ill and it seemed like something we could entertain in the future. Well, now it's the future, and I have to do something.

A few well-meaning people suggested I sell the place and

downsize, but I just can't even think of that. Lavender Valley Farm is my home. I've lived here for almost fifty years and I'm not sure my heart could survive losing my dear Chuck and the only home I've known. Not to mention, all the sweet dogs I've come to think of as my own.

It wasn't often, but Chuck would sometimes put his foot down when I would tell him about one more poor dog that needed a home. Now, without anyone to talk sense into me, I can imagine even more dogs and animals than I ever had.

It seems like when I got too old to foster children, I substituted the furry four-legged variety.

I hope you are doing well and if you take a trip this summer, be sure to stop by. I'd love to see you and Lee.

Much love,
    Jewel

MAY 15, 2021

Dear Georgia,

I hope this letter finds you and Lee well. I've got exciting news to share!
 My neighbor surprised me with a new puppy. I've named her Hope and she's a gorgeous golden retriever. I made the mistake of thinking I was too old for another puppy after Scarlett died. I think he knew I was missing my old girl, gone almost two years now, and when he showed up at my door with this bundle of joy, I was smitten.
 I'm sure people think I'm nuts, since I have so many rescue dogs, but those are here temporarily. Some stay years, but my goal is to find them forever homes with the right people.
 I've always had one or two goldens of my own and like my sweet boy Beau did all those years ago, they help to welcome the newcomers and calm them.
 I wasn't sure I could handle a puppy, but Hope has been a dream and such a comfort to me. So, I'm inundating

everyone with a quick note and a photo of my new girl. I can't resist sharing my happy news.

I'm sure Hope and I will find lots of things to do on the farm together, and she's already proven to be sweet with the other animals. She also loves sitting on my lap and cuddling. I think we're going to be quite the team.

Sending love and doggie kisses your way,
    Jewel

JUNE 5, 2022

Dear Georgia,

I was so sorry to learn of Lee's passing. You have my sincere sympathies. I know how hard it is when the man you've spent most of your life with is gone. The pain is sometimes unbearable and I still have my days when I miss Chuck so much that I can hardly bear it.

You've always had the kindest heart and are such a caretaker to others. Lee couldn't have asked for anyone better than you to be by his side during his illness.

Sixty-two is far too young, believe me. I'm almost eighty-two now; sixty sounds like a youngster to me. After my Chuck left this earth, I wasn't sure I could keep up with things, but like always, God sent me the answer. So many kind people pitched in to help keep me and this old place afloat. I believe that the kind people in Boise will do the same for you.

Writing this to you an old memory bubbled to the surface: the first day you came to live with us. You were so shy and scared. It broke my heart. I tried to get you to eat and you kept saying you weren't hungry. But I knew better. I finally won you over with my brown sugar toast. Do you remember that?

I don't have much of an appetite lately and I haven't made it for years, but now that I'm thinking about it, I might have to soften some butter and toast some bread. Chuck loved it with a scoop of vanilla ice cream on top.

Make some for yourself, and when you eat it, imagine a big hug from me with every sweet bite.

The animals need me, so I'm going to trudge forward as long as I'm blessed to be here. I wish you peace and comfort as you grieve for Lee and find your way.

If you ever need me, I'm only a phone call away.

With much love,
Jewel

OLIVIA

MAY 1980

JEWEL'S JOURNAL

Oh, Olivia! Mrs. Parsons thinks I have a way with teenage girls. I'm not sure about that, but I hope she's right, especially since Chuck and I decided we wanted to open our home to children who were at least school age and leave the babies and infants to others.

All I can say is you make Georgia look like a chatterbox. I hope I can earn your trust, like I did hers. I know it takes time and most likely something other than talking to get you to connect with me.

I just have to figure out what that is.

The way you took to my old friend, Beau, makes me think it might be through our shared love of animals. When I looked in on you tonight, I couldn't bring myself to shoo him off your bed. You need him with you on your first night here.

I admit I'm a bit worried about that large burn on your arm. Mrs. Parsons said you got it from boiling water. She coordinated an appointment with the clinic in Medford and it sounds like we'll be going there on a regular basis, until it's healed.

The last thing I want to do is cause you any pain, so I hope the instructions for treating it at home are easy for me to do. I guess we'll find out tomorrow at the appointment.

Some of the children under our care are only here for a short time, but like with Georgia, Mrs. Parsons tells me you'll be here until you're eighteen, unless it doesn't work out between us. That means I have five years to show you what it means to be loved.

It breaks my heart that you have no family to turn to, but Chuck and I will do our very best to make you feel welcome and part of our family. I know your beautiful blue eyes have seen more heartache than they should have.

I've been hinting to Chuck about rescuing dogs long enough that he's finally building me a nice shelter to make my dream a reality. He's expanding and remodeling that little shed off the back yard and it's going to be wonderful.

There are so many dogs that need a little love and care before they can hope to find their forever homes. I think you might be the helper I need to get my idea off the ground.

I'm anxious to find out, and to nurture what brings you joy.

APRIL 1981

JEWEL'S JOURNAL

Today was one of my favorite days with you, Olivia. I finally saw pure joy in your face when we made the trip to the animal shelter. You've been working hard helping get the sanctuary building ready, and today, we picked up our first two rescues. Those stunning blue eyes of yours finally sparkled.

Like you, I wanted to take them all, but made a promise to Chuck that I'd start with two and see how it went. He's so good to me and indulges all my big ideas, so I'll honor his wishes, for now.

I even heard you giggle when the dogs licked your face. I love that sound and hope to hear more of it. I'm not sure I'm going to be able to get you to sleep in your room after agreeing to let you stay with the new dogs tonight. Good thing it's a weekend and almost summer vacation. Not that the sanctuary isn't comfy and clean, especially with Chuck's built-in little cubby with the bed. I think he must have guessed we might be spending a few nights in there, comforting our furry guests.

I think you're the exact person they need to get them acclimated. We want them to feel safe and secure in their little stable, and then we'll work on socializing them and training them to be good family members in the house.

Your excitement at being put in charge of caring for them and cleaning the sanctuary made my heart leap with happiness. I first noticed that soft heart of yours when you asked to stay with Chuck's horse when it had that little cut from the wire fence. You tended to him with such gentle hands and spoke so sweetly to him. Spirit is a beauty, but definitely Chuck's horse, and doesn't normally take to strangers. With you, it was different. He trusted you, instinctually. I think you might end up being a veterinarian.

Even though your burn is healed, I see how much the scar bothers you and how you always try to wear a long-sleeved shirt to cover it. We'll keep putting that special cream on it and I hope it fades with time. Even more, I hope the emotional pain associated with it fades even quicker. The best thing about dogs is they don't judge us by our looks or imperfections.

I have a surprise I'm trying to keep a secret, but am bursting to share. With my sweet Beau getting older, I'm getting a new puppy from the same breeder. I love goldens and can't imagine my life without one. My new pup will be here in a few months and I'm hoping I can keep quiet about her and surprise you.

I'm going to sneak out and check on you one more time before I turn in tonight. I'm sure I'll find you and my sweet Beau cuddled up with those two dogs.

JULY 1981

JEWEL'S JOURNAL

Oh Olivia, what an adventure it has been. It sure didn't take us long to wear Chuck down and fill up all eight stalls in the sanctuary. We've got two prospective families coming tomorrow, and I have a good feeling that they'll go home with a new best friend. Our lives will be a little easier then, at least until two more pups need our help.

Those dogs are a ton of work, and I'm not sure I could keep up without you. Your idea of reading books to the shelter dogs is pure genius. They love it and it's great practice for the other children in our care. It's summer now, so you have the time, but when school starts up again, we may have to cut back. I'm not sure I can manage things without you.

You've made so much progress, Olivia. I credit the dogs for helping you more than anything else. They've given you a real sense of purpose, and you have a special way with the ones who are hurt or suffering and need a bit of extra care. Like Spirit, they seem to trust you immediately.

My sweet boy Beau has adapted to his role as big brother

to Willow. You came up with a wonderful name for my new girl. She's a total snuggle bug and loves you beyond measure.

I was thrilled to see you ride my horse, Starlight, with Chuck today. Watching you ride, the wind blowing in your hair, and that huge smile on your face made my day. Chuck says you ride like a pro.

I looked in on you on my way to bed tonight and noticed Beau and Willow both on your bed. I think I've created a monster.

MAY 1985

JEWEL'S JOURNAL

I can't believe you're graduating tomorrow, Olivia. The girl who would barely say a word to me five years ago has transformed into such a lovely young woman, not to mention tall and beautiful beyond words. I hate that you're going to be so far away, but at the same time I'm bursting with pride that you've earned a scholarship to Walla Walla University. Your choice to pursue nursing is perfect.

I've already planted the seed with Chuck that we could drive you to school if he gets just one day off work. I love Walla Walla and haven't visited for years. The downtown area is quaint and filled with wonderful shops and old brick buildings. I know you'll love it.

I'm trying to figure out how I can possibly keep up my rescue work without you. I think I'll scale back for a bit, as I don't want to shortchange the dogs—and if we're going to make a trip to Walla Walla, I don't want to overwhelm Mr. Nolan, who is always kind about sending his ranch hands over to help when we need it.

I'm not sure Willow is going to survive your departure.

After Beau passed, I think she became even more attached to you. I'll miss you terribly too, Olivia, but couldn't be happier to see you spread your wings and soar. I know you'll do great things.

    You've made us so proud, sweet girl.

APRIL 5, 1989

Dear Olivia,

We were thrilled to get your college graduation announcement! I'm so sorry we couldn't make the trip, but Chuck couldn't get any time off work. You are going to be a wonderful nurse, and it's fantastic that you already have a job.

We've enclosed a check and hope you use it for something fun to celebrate your huge achievement. When you were young, I thought you might pursue a veterinary degree, since you were always caring for the animals, but a nurse is a perfect fit for you. You were the first one to jump in and help whenever anybody had a cut or needed a sliver removed.

You are a natural, and you'll be a shining star at the hospital in Spokane. I'm sure your work schedule will be hectic, but if you get some time off, I hope you'll come and visit us on the farm.

As you know, I was so sad when we lost our sweet Willow earlier this year. I know you felt her loss deeply too. When you come visit, I'll introduce you to my newest golden, Daisy. May she mend your heart as she is mending mine. I've enclosed a photo I think you'll enjoy.

We'd love to see you and hear all about your new job.

With all our love,
    Jewel and Chuck

MARCH 20, 1996

Dear Olivia,

Congratulations on the birth of your son. I was so happy to receive the announcement. Simon is quite handsome, and what a head of hair! I know you'll be a wonderful mother. I have fond memories of you taking such good care of all the animals. There was more than one morning I found you had stayed in the barn all night with a goat or a horse who wasn't feeling well, willing them better with your soft heart and gentle touch. It's no wonder you're a fabulous nurse.

I'm glad you're taking some time from work to stay home with your sweet boy. Children are the most precious gift we can receive and you'll never regret the time you spend with him.

I wish we lived closer. I would love to come and help you and cuddle little Simon.

I've already added his baby picture to the mantle and hope you'll send me more as he grows. Nothing brings me more happiness than seeing my kids thrive and have families of their own.

I'm not the best knitter, but I did manage to make a blanket, and I hope that when you use it, you'll think of me and know how much I love you and little Simon. Give my best to Glen. I'm sure he's a proud daddy.

With love and best wishes,
    Jewel and Chuck

MARCH 9, 2009

Dear Olivia,

I love the photos you sent in your last letter. You look so beautiful in your nurse's uniform. Congratulations on your big promotion. Your dark hair under that white hat is striking. I know most nurses don't wear the white hat and uniform nowadays, but I wish they did.

When Chuck was unwell and we spent so much time with doctors and in hospitals, it was the nurses that made it bearable. Good ones have a wonderful impact on patients and their families. I can imagine you are one of the best and now in your new role, you'll be able to instill that in the younger nurses. I saw that quality in you at a young age. You have a gentle way with anyone in pain and suffering. Chuck and I often talked about you, and when we had an exceptional nurse, would always imagine she was just like you.

The family photo is also lovely. Simon looks so grown up at just 13 years. Love all those happy smiles. I've added it to my bookcase so I can see you when I pass by it each day.

My favorite photo is the one in your front yard, showcasing all that snow Spokane received. It's unbelievable. I think we get about four inches a year here and you get more than four feet! It's beautiful, but I'd rather not have to shovel it.

I know it's a long trip to visit, but if you ever get down this way, I'd love to see you.

All my love,
    Jewel

JANUARY 5, 2021

Dear Olivia,

I am absolutely heartbroken for you. I read your letter about Simon going to prison, and I've been searching for the right words to comfort you. I know how much you love him and how hard you've worked to help him.

I'm sure you're shattered, and I worry so much about you, my sweet girl. Your heart was always so tender and I know it is broken in a million pieces. I wish there was something I could do for you to make this better.

I do hope he gets out in less than two years, like you said the lawyer suspected. I pray he's safe and finds someone that leads him in the right direction, away from more sadness and despair. I hope there is a support group he can attend there.

We've had children in our care who had drug problems, and they were some of the hardest to help. As a mother, I know you want to fix things for him, and that it is tearing you apart to be powerless to do so.

I will add Simon to my prayers and keep you close in thought as you come to grips with all of this.

With all my love,
    Jewel

MARCH 2, 2022

Dear Olivia,

I'm so glad to know Simon was released early. I'm sure you are relieved. I do hope he listens to you, stays connected to that support group, and attends his meetings. I think the struggle is so very difficult and hard to overcome.

    Like alcoholism, I think it's a life-long battle and people swear by the groups and meetings, so I do hope that helps Simon. He couldn't have a better champion than you. Like you, I'd want to wrap him in bubble-wrap and keep him locked in his room where he's safe, but life doesn't work that way, does it?

    I've prayed for him daily and will continue to keep him in my prayers. Like you mentioned, trying to find a job after prison isn't easy, and I hope he can find a good one where he's surrounded by strong role models.

    I'm including a photo of my sweet girl, Hope. She's the light of my life and my constant companion. More like a shadow. She never leaves my side. There is nothing like the bond of a dog. It truly is unbreakable and never faltering. I hope the photo of Hope smiling makes you smile, dear girl.

Please remember, in the midst of taking care of everyone else, be kind to yourself and rest.

With love,
Jewel

SEPTEMBER 9, 2022

Dear Olivia,

I am truly heartbroken at your news of Simon's passing. I don't know what to say or do for you. I'm not sure how a mother survives the loss of a child, no matter the age of her child.

I know how much hope you held for Simon, and that you thought he was on the right path. Mothers always blame themselves and I got a sense of that in your short letter. Olivia, my sweet girl, I beg of you not to carry the burden for this.

You did everything in your power to help your boy. I know you did. Drugs are a scourge on our entire society and destroy so many lives. I'm just so sorry Simon and you, along with Glen, were victims to the horror.

The journey of grief is different for everyone, so don't let anyone tell you what is normal. You mentioned going back to work and if that gives you respite, do it. If you feel better staying home, do that. Surround yourself with people that make you feel better, and find things to occupy your time that bring you happiness, even if only for a few minutes.

I added you to our prayer chain, and I hope it comforts you to know that so many people will be praying and thinking of you. I wish I could take away your pain.

If you need a soft shoulder, I'm here for you.

Love and prayers for you,
Jewel

HARRY

SEPTEMBER 1985

JEWEL'S JOURNAL

Harriet, or Harry as you told me you like to be called, you came through my door today, and unlike the other children I've had in my care, Mrs. Parsons told me your history. I'm so very sorry you lost both of your parents in a car accident so long ago. I'm glad your grandma was able to take you in, but from what Mrs. Parsons said, I have a feeling you've been a caretaker during the year before she passed. I hope you can find some happiness and rest under our roof.

I guess because your parents and grandma are gone, Mrs. Parsons can share more. It finally hit me that if the parents are still in the picture somehow, she doesn't divulge much about the history of the children. I guess there is some confidentiality issue, but it would truly help me to know more about what's happened in the past. Speaking of Mrs. Parsons, I can't say I'm sorry to hear she's retiring. I do wish her all the best and understand her job is difficult, but I'm looking forward to working with a new case manager.

I was so thankful to hear you didn't come from an abusive situation. In my experience, it's harder to build trust with those children. She tells me you're an excellent student too, but one without hobbies.

I'm hopeful we can make a connection and find something you enjoy. I'm also happy you won't have to move on, unless it's your choice. I've so enjoyed the extended years I've been able to spend with some of the other children who have been in my care. They hold a special place in my heart, and I have a feeling you will too.

You have an air of confidence about you, which I love to see, and you're not timid and shy like so many of the other children. With what's happened, I'm sure you've had to grow up too fast.

I was happy to see how gentle you were with Willow. She's a love bug and along with her, I'll introduce you to the rescue dogs and the other animals on the farm. I found it interesting that she didn't climb up on your bed tonight. Dogs are so in tune with us, and I'm going to take that as a good sign that she knows you don't need the extra support she normally offers to our new arrivals. I did find her sprawled in front of your bedroom door when I was on my way to bed, so she wants to keep you safe, but respects your need for space. She's smart like that, and something tells me you're very special.

FEBRUARY 1986

JEWEL'S JOURNAL

I must say, Harry, I've never met a more organized and focused teenager. I never have to ask you if your homework is done, and you pitch in to do the laundry and other chores without me even asking. I appreciate that so much, and I hope you enjoy that set of Sue Grafton mystery books that are my thank you gift for all that you do around here.

I spied them at the library sale, and when I found out you hadn't read them yet, I knew I had to get them for you. When I checked on you tonight, it made me so happy to see you engrossed in the first book, and the big smile you gave me was magical.

Your smiles are far too rare. I sometimes feel like you're already grown-up, even though you're just fourteen now. You're more like fourteen going on forty. I sometimes forget you're not my friend. Honestly, I think you're more mature than most of the women I know.

Outside of puzzles and mystery novels, or watching *Murder She Wrote* and *Cagney and Lacey*, I haven't been able to find much that puts a sparkle in your eye. I saw a hint of one the other night though, when you discovered Chuck's old chess set in the hall closet. Already, you're so good at it. I think I'll ask you to teach me how to play.

You're good with the animals too, especially Willow, and never fail to handle the chores, but I can see you do everything from a sense of duty, not joy. I do think you enjoy reading to the shelter dogs and it's wonderful to watch them respond to your voice.

With your intelligence, quick wit, and ability to tackle any task, I do wonder what you'll be drawn to for a career. I haven't figured it out, but I have a few more years.

MARCH 1989

JEWEL'S JOURNAL

I guess I should have seen it coming, Harry. Today when you got home from school, I've never seen you so excited. The job shadow you did with the police detective in Medford cinched your plan to go into law enforcement.

I don't think you've ever talked at the dinner table as much as you did tonight. I finally had to get up and get the two sisters to their baths. You held our attention for two whole hours with all the exciting things you learned and did over the last two days with Detective Warren.

He sounds like a wonderful person, and I'm so glad your teacher recommended you for the program. I think you've found your calling, my dear one.

I have a feeling you'll have those applications for scholarships filled out before the week is over. Detective Warren's advice about getting a start with studying criminology and then going to the academy when you're twenty-one makes great sense. I'm even more thrilled that he's willing to sponsor you in so many programs to get your degree covered.

I guess all those mystery books paid off, didn't they? I'm so happy to see you truly excited and looking forward to the future. I want nothing more than to see you doing something you love, something that fulfills you.

I noticed your light was still on tonight when I went to bed, and I kept right on walking by your room. It would be an exercise in futility to ask you to stop reading through all that information Detective Warren gave you.

I've got to get to sleep, but I do so with a lighter heart, knowing you're on a path that suits you to a "T."

MAY 10, 1992

Dear Harry,

I know we just saw you at your graduation, but I couldn't resist writing to tell you again how much we enjoyed our time. We are bursting at the seams with pride. You are going to make a wonderful police officer, intelligent, just, and brave. You were always a rule follower and liked order, plus you were smart as a whip and could solve any puzzle. You weren't easy to fool, and you kept your eye on some of the other kids who could be more than mischievous, passing along information you thought we needed to know to keep them safe.

I showed your graduation program to two of the girls we have staying with us now, and they were so impressed that you're a police officer. One of them is a real handful, so I was hoping it might serve as a deterrent if she knew I had a policewoman in the family. Say a prayer for me.

Chuck and I had a fabulous time playing hooky and staying at the wonderful hotel you recommended. It's not often that we can get away from the farm, but the trip to Salem was lovely and we completely enjoyed seeing you decked out in your uniform. What an honor to be sitting among all those proud parents.

I'm relieved to know you'll be working in Salem. It's a big enough city, but seems safer than the Portland option. We still worry about you, no matter how old you are. Be safe and come to visit when you can.

We loved being part of your special ceremony and know you will do great things. Thank you again for inviting us. It was wonderful to see you so happy and fulfilled.

With all our love,
   Jewel and Chuck

FEBRUARY 23, 2001

Dear Harry,

Well, I'm sixty-one years old this year, and it's time to hang up my foster-mom hat. Our case manager didn't actually say we were too old, but she hinted at it. Honestly, as much joy and fulfillment all the children we've fostered have brought us, I'm ready to turn the page.

I don't think we're meant to have teenagers in our sixties. We can't keep up with them and we need some rest. I looked back in my notebook and couldn't believe we've been doing this for almost thirty years. I was thirty-three when I welcomed our first foster-child, Georgia, into our home.

We were so nervous and didn't know what we were doing. Chuck and I just knew we had lots of love to give and wanted to help as many children as possible. It wasn't always easy, but I have no regrets. We just said goodbye to the last young lady to live under our roof. Micki is her name and her life wasn't easy, but she's another smart one and helped me so much in the flower garden.

I'm not much for computers, but Micki loved them and could master anything on them. We had to get one for the children to do their homework and projects, so it sits in the den and I snarl at it when I walk by. I'll miss Micki since she always jumped at the chance to look up anything I needed online. She told me it's not going away and I need to learn it, but I'm still resisting.

With Chuck retired and all our home improvement and remodeling projects completed, and now sending our last little one on her way into adulthood, we hope to be able to take a few trips and enjoy the years we have left. The animals complicate taking much of a vacation, but our neighbor is good about lending us some of his ranch hands when we need help.

We've got a trip planned to go over to the coast and I'm looking forward to that. I think I've got Chuck talked into going to the Iris Festival in May and if we do, we can pop over and visit you in Salem. I'll keep you posted.

Thank you too for the beautiful birthday card! Chuck treated me to a lovely dinner in town and the most delicious cake, but now that we're childless, the real celebration will happen in Bandon. That's where we honeymooned, so it's a special spot for us.

Sending love, and hope to see you soon,
    Jewel & Chuck

JANUARY 7, 2003

Dear Harry,

We had such a lovely visit with you. Chuck and I were so surprised when you showed up at the door the day after Christmas. It was the highlight of our year to have you spend a few days at the farm, plus the best gift ever!

    I loved introducing you to my new pup, Scarlett. I've never had a golden as red as she is, but I think she's gorgeous. My sweet Daisy passed away a few months ago and like I've done ever since I had a golden, I made sure to get a puppy when my older dog was around to help train her. Daisy did a good job, and I think Scarlett will be a fabulous companion.

    I know how hard it is for you to get away from work, so taking the time to drive down here means the world to us. After you left, Chuck told me how he wished he lived closer, so he could help you with some of your home improvement projects. We enjoyed seeing all the photos of your home.

Your house is lovely, and the plans you have for it are fabulous.

I think I enjoyed our walk around the property and sitting in front of the fire late into the evening, just talking, the very most. I've missed our chats. My eyes aren't as good as they were when you lived here, but I had such fun working that new puzzle with you. Thank you again for bringing it.

I still feel horrible that I didn't have a gift for you, after you showered us with such decadent treats. Those cupcakes you brought us were the best I ever tasted. Not to mention the socks and slippers you brought for each of us. They are so warm and comfy, and I've been wearing them nonstop since I opened them.

I'm embarrassed that dinner at the Grasshopper and a marionberry pie are all we could offer you in return.

We hope you'll come to visit again soon. We are so proud of you and all you've done with your life.

Hugs and love,
    Jewel and Chuck

APRIL 30, 2008

Dear Harry,

Just a quick note to let you know how much it meant to me that you came to visit and attend the service for Chuck. I know it's not easy for you to get away, and it was wonderful to have you here, especially at such a low point in my life.

I promise to take you up on your offer to check out anyone I want to hire as a farmhand. Like you said, it's important to be careful and not be so trusting, now that I'm on my own.

At least with all the animals, I have a built-in alarm system and luckily, Lavender Valley is still small and relatively crime-free. I've always loved it here and enjoy the close-knit community, but everyone turning out for Chuck and offering their help to me, made me realize how very lucky I am to live here.

I'm trying to adjust to this new normal, but it's difficult. Thank goodness for my dogs and other animals, since they keep me busy and always manage to make me laugh. They also force me to get out of bed, which lately has become harder. Grief comes in waves and it's hardest first thing in the morning and late at night. It's when I miss Chuck the most.

Thankfully, my neighbor that owns the acreage next door has been nice enough to send some of his workers over to help me. I don't want to take advantage of his kindness, so will make finding a permanent solution a priority this coming week. I'll be in touch with a name and information as soon as I have it. I've got your business card on my refrigerator.

In the meantime, I'm going to make some of my famous pies and take them to my neighbor to thank him and all the men who came to my rescue.

I hope to see you again soon, and know that I think of you often. Lately, I've longed for the days gone by, when you were young, and the house was filled with children, and Chuck and I were so very happy.

Getting old is not for the faint of heart.

Sending you all my love,
    Jewel

APRIL 10, 2015

Dear Harry,

I've followed your career from afar, proud of all your promotions as you moved up in the ranks. I know how hard it was for you to keep up with your work and get your Master's degree at the same time.

I've often read your name in the newspapers and even caught a glimpse of you on the news. Now, I see you've been promoted to Deputy Chief of Investigations. Wow!

I think you are the most independent young woman I ever had under my roof and possibly the smartest. I'm so proud of you, Harry, and all the good you've done in this crazy world of ours. You were always curious and looking to right the wrongs. I love seeing you doing this now and helping those who need it most.

Remember all those hours we played puzzles and read mysteries? You were always so thoughtful in solving them, so I'm not surprised you've risen so high in the detective ranks. Salem is lucky to have you.

My only regret is that you aren't closer, so we could visit more often. I know you're busy and it's tough to make the trip, but I do miss you. I don't get away from Lavender Valley much. There's too much work to do and it's hard to find someone to take care of the animals.

Things are busy here at the farm. You'll remember my dog rescue project, I'm sure. Well, let's just say it's grown. My flower garden hobby has also morphed into a nice little business. The Lavender Festival in July is a huge money maker for the farm and keeps me quite busy.

I can't do as much as I used to, so have had to hire some temporary help during the busy season. I still tend to my chores each day, just not as quickly and not as long as I did when I was younger.

They say, "move it or lose it," right? I'm still moving it, just slower. I hope you can make it down for a visit soon.

Love to you,
Jewel

DECEMBER 22, 2022

Dear Harry,

Thank you so much for the wonderful basket of holiday treats. I'm trying to limit myself to only one sweet a day and typically have something with a cup of tea in the evening.

I hope you were able to get some time off during the holidays. I know crime never takes a day off, and I think you told me once that you're actually busier around the holidays. That's a shameful thought for our society.

The holidays always bring on a bit of regret and nostalgia for me. I long for the days when Chuck and I had a houseful of children. Christmas was always such a magical time, and we tried to make it special for each of the children in our care, even if they were only here for a short time.

Now, I do my best to make it special for all the dogs and the other animals that call Lavender Valley Farm home. I've included a photo of the dogs decked out in their cute bandanas and reindeer antler headbands. Aren't they the cutest?

Marcie, down at the quilt shop, made Christmas pajamas for the baby goats, and they are too cute for words. I was able to get Santa hats on my two alpacas. At least for a few minutes!

It's raining and I'm sitting by the fire, getting more tired as I write this. You might even have a hard time reading my handwriting. It used to be so perfect and these last few years, it's gotten worse.

As I sit here, my sweet girl Hope is next to me. You know I love all my dogs, but I do believe goldens are one of the best breeds, and Hope may be my favorite dog yet. She's been by my side these last two years and was the perfect welcomer for all the newbies that I have taken in. Unfortunately, this last year, I've slowed down, and now I'm no longer accepting new rescues. I just don't have the energy.

I would love to see you soon, Harry. Know that I think of you often and my heart swells with pride when I do.

Much love,
    Jewel

LYDIA

AUGUST 1990

JEWEL'S JOURNAL

Oh, my goodness, Lydia. I think you're going to be more than a handful. Maybe I'm just getting too old for teenage girls. I don't think so, though. I think you might be protecting yourself and that's why you're a bit snippy and impolite. Some of my rescue dogs do the same thing.

Trust me, I won't give up on you and I'm not going anywhere.

Ms. Phelps, who is a breath of fresh air after dealing with Mrs. Parsons, told me I should plan on fostering you for the next five years, as your mother is in jail and you never knew your father. I'm sure both of those facts are embarrassing for you and I won't be bringing them up to you.

Your blue eyes hold so much despair, it breaks my heart. You remind me of one of the rescues I just placed with a wonderful family. His name is Humphrey and he had no confidence when he arrived, matted and full of fleas. He'd been neglected and worse, I fear.

It took some time, but he came to trust me, and my patience paid off as he became very attached to me. It was hard to let him go, but his new family is perfect and loving, and he will have the life he deserves.

I'm going to give you plenty of space and support, and together we'll find a way to connect. I can't wait for hope to replace the sadness in your eyes. When I helped you with your beautiful blonde hair tonight, I noticed you flinch at my touch. It broke my heart.

The first thing I'm going to do is find you some suitable clothes. Everything we unpacked is torn or frayed or way too small. School starts soon, and I think we're going to have to go shopping to find you some new things, especially shoes and a warm coat.

I'm going to let Ms. Phelps know I need to concentrate on you, so I don't want to take in anyone else for a few months. I think you need all of my attention. I also think I need to keep my eye on you. You're not going to make it easy, but I think you'll be worth the effort.

Rest easy on your first night, sweet girl. I did see your kindness shine through when you bent and touched your forehead to my sweet Daisy's. She's the best balm to heal the wounds of the new children who come to stay with us.

You can also tell her anything. She's a great listener and keeps all my secrets.

FEBRUARY 1992

JEWEL'S JOURNAL

Today is my birthday, and I don't think I've ever eaten a more delicious and gorgeous cake. Usually, it's one or the other. Pretty, but tasteless, or yummy and a little on the ugly side. Lydia, yours was simply divine.

You even decorated it with my favorite lavender flowers, and though I've never had a lavender buttercream frosting, now I'm not sure I can live without it.

My heart is full, not just because of the wonderful birthday you helped me celebrate, but because I've witnessed such a transformation in you, my sweet girl.

Had you told me two years ago that you'd be smiling and spending hours in the kitchen making us delicious treats and meals, without a complaint, I probably wouldn't have believed it.

Your talent is remarkable, especially for someone so young. I think you've made every recipe in those cookbooks we got you for Christmas. I guess I'll have to find more for this year. Someday, my claim to fame will be that I taught Lydia, the famous chef, how to make marionberry jam. I'm sure the student will surpass the teacher in that department soon.

Chuck told me he wants a chocolate cake for his birthday, so you've got some time to come up with a new masterpiece.

This is a birthday I'll cherish forever.

MAY 1995

JEWEL'S JOURNAL

I won't say you made it easy, my dear Lydia, but I am sad to see you leave us. The first few months with you were a bit of a struggle, but when I figured out you thrived in the kitchen, our lives became easier.

I will miss your wonderful meals and all the fun we had creating new dishes together. I'm not a stellar cook. I've always enjoyed baking, but not so much the drudgery of cooking regular meals. I know the shelter dogs are going to miss your homemade dog cookies, too.

With you, it became a highlight in my day. Probably because you did most of it and meals that you thought up were so unique and tasty. Chuck is going to be back to my boring fare now.

You have a true gift and are so creative. Your counselor told us how hard it is to get into the culinary school. I had no idea they took so few students. We couldn't be prouder of your perseverance. I know how hard you worked to keep your grades up, which was especially challenging while getting the required experience working at the Sugar Shack.

Your hard work paid off! To get a scholarship is rare, and yet you wowed them with your dishes and were awarded the coveted full-ride.

I'm even more happy that you've found joy and are out from under the dark cloud that was hanging over you when you first arrived. Like I've told you so many times, you are not your mother. You have a pathway to success doing something you truly love.

I dream of coming to eat at your restaurant when you're a full-fledged chef. I can't wait to see what you do in the future, and I know that whatever it is, it will be spectacular.

JUNE 30, 1996

Dear Lydia,

Chuck retired from the road department a few weeks ago, and I hosted a huge party for him at the farm. It made me think of you and wish you were here to help with the food. I tried to replicate that wonderful potato salad you make with the fresh lemon and mustard dressing. It was tasty, but yours was better.

I can't even begin to rival you in the baking department, so opted to have Aimee at the bakery handle the cakes and treats. She did a fabulous job and said to tell you hello.

I think the entire town of Lavender Valley showed up to honor Chuck. He smiled all afternoon and everyone stayed late. We even had live music, courtesy of the band made up of local teachers.

All his coworkers and his boss came. Chuck will miss seeing them each day, but I don't think he'll miss the work. We've always been thankful that he took that job when we first married, and it was a good career for him. The little we make at the farm would never have sustained us, but his work, though not always exciting or fun, gave us a steady income over all these years.

I'm trying to convince him to enjoy his retirement years and to not overwork himself on the farm. We'll see how that goes. First on his list is a big remodel, and I'm getting a dream kitchen. I can't wait for you to see it when it's done.

I hope you're doing well and enjoying your studies at the culinary school. I'm so excited to see where you end up after you graduate. If you have time to sneak down for a visit before you start work, we'd love to see you.

Sending lots of love,
   Jewel and Chuck

JUNE 30, 2000

Dear Lydia,

I'm enclosing a few photos of my new kitchen. I know you will appreciate the double ovens and the huge granite counter. I sure could have used all this when we had a houseful of kids, but I'm in love with it now too.

Now, all I need is you to come to visit and test it out. Chuck has been working hard, not only on the kitchen, but giving our bathrooms an upgrade and new flooring throughout the house. Lots of painting, and I almost forgot, a new roof.

It's been crazy, but the end result is heavenly. He's even got a bee in his bonnet and is working on updating the cottages and barn. By the time he's done, everything will be new and improved, plus he's enjoying it and it keeps him busy.

He's been good about getting in some subcontractors to help with things that are too cumbersome, and we've been saving up a long time to get this done. We just never had the time to do it.

I tried that truffle oil and the recipes you included in your last package. It's so good. You know Chuck is not very adventurous when it comes to food, but he loved the truffled mushroom with prosciutto and taleggio grilled cheese. To be fair, I won him over with the truffle mac and cheese first, and then tried the more exotic recipe.

We think of you often and would love to have you visit soon.

Much love,
    Jewel and Chuck

MARCH 1, 2003

Dear Lydia,

It sounds like you are getting lots of experience working in Portland. And, you've still got enough energy to be a partner in a food cart business. I admit, that's something I've only heard about. It sounds intriguing and like a low overhead way to start a business. When you first mentioned it, I pictured a roll around cart that you push, and couldn't for the life of me figure that one out. Then, when you explained it was an actual food truck, and that they call them carts in Portland, it made more sense.

I can't imagine so many carts in the Pioneer Courthouse Square and to think you sell out each day for lunch. I shouldn't be surprised, but that's amazing. It's very smart to have a limited menu. That would help keep things simple and costs down.

I love grilled cheese, and the menu you sent with your last letter made my mouth water. I think Chuck would be a big fan of the slow roasted barbecued pork with two kinds of cheese on the parmesan crusted bread. You also can't go wrong with the bacon version. Offering homemade tomato soup is the perfect side.

I'm making myself hungry writing this. When you come to visit next, I think I'll ask you to make us some.

So happy to know you're doing well and can't wait to see you.

Much love,
    Jewel and Chuck

FEBRUARY 21, 2013

Dear Lydia,

I've been tuning into the Portland channel to watch you in the local baking competition. After watching these last weeks and rooting for you each time, I went to the Sugar Shack to view the final competition. Aimee's daughter now runs it, and she was so proud to tell everyone you started your baking career right here in Lavender Valley.

She had quite a crowd, and we all nibbled on some of her yummy cupcakes while we watched. We were so nervous, and when they announced you as the winner, the crowd roared with applause. I'm surprised you didn't hear us from Portland. I wish Chuck could have been here to see that. He'd be so proud, just like I am.

There are signs and banners in all the store windows congratulating you. I think you'll have celebrity following the next time you come to town.

Those desserts they had you making looked so difficult

and you hardly had time to do it. I'm not sure how you managed it all, but somehow you made it look easy.

I hope you'll find time to visit soon. I'd love to bake something with you.

All my love,
    Jewel

OCTOBER 29, 2017

Dear Lydia,

How are you, dear? I cut out your picture from the newspaper and have it on my bookcase. I'm so proud of all you've accomplished. Head chef at such a fancy place in Portland!

Not that I had any doubts, you were destined for great things, but it was lovely to open the paper and see your pretty face. Those food critics waxed on about all your dishes. Honestly, I don't know what some of them even were, but I'm sure they're divine.

I've been making lots of your famous potato soup these days, but yours is always better than mine.

Have you made any jam lately? I'm making marionberry again this year. I think it's my absolute favorite, but if you have any new ones to try, send them along. You had a knack for combining things to make the most delicious jam. If only I had some of your homemade bread to go with it. Alas, I'll have to make do with mine.

If you get down my way, I hope you'll stop in. No need to call, just show up. I'm always home and would love to see you.

Sending love to you,
    Jewel

NOVEMBER 1, 2021

Dear Lydia,

I hope this finds you well. Actually, I hope it finds you at all. I've sent a few letters over the last few months and they keep coming back to me, undeliverable. I know you have a wandering spirit, but I would love to keep in touch with you.

Better yet, bring that little motorhome you love and visit the farm. I'd love to see you. Maybe I could talk you into cooking something fabulous for me. The last time I knew where you were, it was on the coast in Brookings.

I still remember when you first asked me if you could cook. I admit, I was skeptical, but once I tasted your concoctions, there was no going back. I loved having you under my roof and in my kitchen. I can only imagine how your natural talent has blossomed.

I always picture you running a kitchen and teaching your young proteges how it's done. What I wouldn't give for one of your homemade chocolates right now. I hate to admit it, but I think my cooking days are behind me. My knees bother me and it's hard to stand and do all the prep and cooking, so I opt for easy meals.

Well, my dear, I hope you are happy, cooking up a storm, and I do hope you'll find time to come to visit and stay for a spell.

Hugs to you,
   Jewel

AUGUST 20, 2022

Dear Lydia,

I just got home having spent some time in the hospital up in Medford. The food was horrible, and I'm sitting here craving a bowl of your delicious soup. The ladies at the church were nice enough to set up meals for me and they bring enough to feed me for a week each day, so I'm not going hungry.

My appetite is not great, but I do dream of your soup. I mentioned soup to one of the ladies and today received a container of a brothy concoction, but it doesn't hold a candle to yours.

I do hope you get this letter, Lydia. I sent it to General Delivery, since that worked the last few times. I worry about you out on the road on your own. I hope you have some good friends to lean on and that you are taking care of yourself.

I know with the weather soon turning colder, it won't be easy to travel, but if you find a few free days, I hope you'll drive over and visit. I promise not to make you cook the whole time you're here.

I feel time slipping away from me and would love to see you before I have to go.

Much love to you,
 Jewel

MICKI

JULY 1995

JEWEL'S JOURNAL

I resisted, but finally caved to Ms. Phelps, and agreed to take one more teenage girl under my wing. She told me about a young girl named Michelle, who liked to be called Micki. Once I heard that you needed a place to call home, Micki, a real home and not just one for just a few months, I knew I couldn't refuse.

I'm too old to take on much more than one child these days, so hopefully you won't mind being my only one. I keep a notebook with the names of all my kids and when they stayed at Lavender Valley Farm. You, my dear, are number fifty-five. I think that's a good number to be the last one.

Now, most of those fifty-five have only spent a short time here, some a few weeks, others several months, and you'll make the fifth young lady to stay for more than a year.

Hopefully, I've learned something over the last twenty years and will be able to figure out what you enjoy and what might speak to you. I have a feeling it might be flowers. I saw the way you gazed at that vase of wildflowers on the table, and you even knew the names of most of them.

I love planting and growing things and have my fingers crossed that I may finally get a child who loves getting her fingers in the dirt. I have big plans to show you my planting room in the cottage and see if it sparks your interest.

You've already made fast friends with Daisy and commented on her name being one of your favorite flowers. I think that's a good sign.

My heart aches for you, dear girl. I noticed the faint color around your brown eyes and recognize an almost healed bruise when I see one. I've seen far too many old bruises on the sweet children I've taken into my home. I didn't mention it, because I'm sure you're not ready to discuss it.

I hope you'll soon realize you're safe here and that you won't suffer any such treatment while you're under our roof. Someday, when you're ready, you can tell me your story, but for now, I just want you to rest and in the coming days we'll work together to find something that piques your interest and brings you joy.

You deserve to be safe and happy and while I can guarantee the first one, I hope you'll let me help you find happiness here on the farm.

AUGUST 1997

JEWEL'S JOURNAL

I've watched you change over this last year. It took some time for you to trust us and heal from the physical wounds you came with and I can tell you're making progress on the emotional scars you carry. When you told me more about your mother and how much you longed for her to love you, my heart broke. I hope you know how much we love you and appreciate you.

I can't believe your energy, Micki. I'm so thankful Chuck is retired and he can help us prepare the ground. My little patch of lavender always grew so well, but when you discovered we had the perfect soil for it, it made sense to expand our thinking and try to grow it for retail purposes.

I'm thrilled at the idea that you helped make a reality and the new field of lavender blooming. I know it will take another year or two until we see the full results, but looking out on that gorgeous purple sea makes my heart so happy. I'm even happier seeing you blossom in front of my eyes as you transform our dirt into something truly beautiful.

I can't wait to see how our sunflowers do. Those will be stunning against the dark wood of the barn.

As reluctant as I was to get a computer, I have to admit it's come in handy for researching flower information. You are such a whiz with it. Your teachers tell me you excel in that realm and have a natural ability in programming.

That's all over my head, but I love seeing you happy and engaged in something you enjoy. I also think it's made a real difference in your attitude at school. I think the idea of losing access to the computer is the stick and also the carrot that works for you.

It sounds like your teachers think you'll have no problem getting a scholarship in that field, and have already mentioned the University of Washington. I saw that little sparkle in your eyes when the counselor talked about that possibility.

You've found your footing, dear one, and so quickly. If anyone can make a career out of computers and flowers, it will be you.

MAY 2000

JEWEL'S JOURNAL

Micki the Magnificent. That's your new name. Chuck and I were so proud to watch you graduate with honors, not to mention having a good portion of your college degree already under your belt.

I'm so thrilled that you were able to get in that program with UW and take those advanced classes. Now, you'll only have to put in one more year and you'll be done, plus you have a guaranteed job.

You are amazing.

While I'm so excited for you to embark on your next chapter, I will miss you so much. Now, Chuck and I are going to tend to all those flower beds by ourselves. The lavender has been outstanding, and I still marvel at your business sense when you suggested raising it and being part of the big Lavender Festival. It has been a nice little boost to our income.

While I'd love to promise we will visit you, Seattle is a long trip, so I'll hold onto the hope that you may decide to visit us one day soon.

You've made my last placement with the foster system a very happy one. I love ending my career on a high note, and love even more seeing you such a success.

NOVEMBER 30, 2002

Dear Micki,

I'm so happy to know you're expecting another baby. How exciting for you, and it will be nice to have them so close together. That way your little Chad will have a built-in playmate. I know it's probably hard for you with Steve deployed. I hope he makes it home for the birth.

I'm enclosing a photo from the dahlia festival we went to this year. It was so worth the trip up north to see this spectacular farm. I've always wanted to grow them, but never found the time. That farm is out of this world.

I remember how much you loved flowers and wondered if you've ever been to the festival. We went in September, and it was perfect.

It's about four hours north of us, and with you being outside of Seattle, it would be a similar trip for you. We should plan to meet there one year!

I'm also so happy the company you work for is letting you work from home. That's a relief for you, I'm sure. I can't imagine trying to work with an infant and being pregnant. But you were also so efficient, so I'm sure you have everything and everyone all organized.

I can't wait to see baby pictures. Be sure to send them along. I enclosed a few dahlia tubers for you to plant this spring.

All my love,
    Jewel

JANUARY 10, 2008

Dear Micki,

I'm so sorry to hear that you lost your husband, and at such a young age. My heart is breaking for you, dear one. I read about the horrific attack in Iraq in the news. I have such admiration for those who choose the military service, and for their families. Your sweet Steve gave the ultimate sacrifice, and it saddens me that you and your two children are left without him. I hope you have help, dear girl.

If only I was younger, I would make the trip to help you, but Chuck is not in the best of health, and it's not something I can handle on my own. With him feeling poorly, I've been having to do more physical work around the farm too. The doctors don't hold out much hope for him, which makes things even harder. I'm just thankful we've had forty-seven years together. What you're facing is so much worse. I can't even imagine. I'm struggling just thinking of not having Chuck here.

Don't be afraid to ask for anything you need. I'm

enclosing a check and I hope it helps you in some way. It's not much, but please use it to ease your burden.

Twenty-five is much too young to have the weight of the world on your shoulders and the responsibility of two young children. Please let me know how you're doing and if you need to talk, please call me. I'm usually indoors during the evening hours. I'm holding you in my thoughts and prayers.

With much love,
    Jewel and Chuck

DECEMBER 1, 2009

Dear Micki,

Just a quick note to check on you and send along a little holiday cheer for you and the children. It can't be easy tending to them and making sure Christmas is special for them, all on your own.

Please use the enclosed to treat them to something extravagant that they want. Since I know you always put them first, I included a gift card for you. I've never had a spa treatment, but I have it on good authority that they are delightful, and I hope you enjoy it.

If you're open to it, I'd love for you and the children to come visit on their spring break. It's a beautiful time at the farm, and would make for an inexpensive vacation for all of you. They could entertain themselves on the farm and play with all the animals, and you could get some rest.

I'd love to see all of you and hope you'll consider it. I admit, I'm feeling a little blue without Chuck. Having you here would be a true gift.

Sending love to you and the children,
 Jewel

AUGUST 30, 2020

Dear Micki,

I love the photos you sent with Meg's high school graduation announcement. She's beautiful, and the picture of the three of you, with Chad looking so grown up and handsome, is front and center on my bookcase. You look wonderful, and should be so proud to have done such a marvelous job raising those two on your own.

Both of them in college, to boot. I'm sure it couldn't have been easy. Maybe now, with them in school, you can take some time for yourself.

Are you still working from home doing that computer work?

I guess I never should have nagged you to get off the computer. It seems like you found a lucrative career. I've never been much for computers, but admire your skill and ability.

With your birds out of the nest, if you get an itch to take a drive, I hope you'll come my way. I even have a wireless connection out here on the farm. Hard to believe, right? We're quite modern now.

I would love to see you and spend some time visiting. My dogs get all my attention, and my farmhand, Tyler, handles all the daily chores. My neighbor, Clay Nolan, has loaned him to me on a permanent basis. I spend most of my time indoors, usually with a dog or two on my lap.

The big lavender festival is over, which is the busiest time here at the farm. Things will quiet down as winter approaches, and then in spring, like the bees and butterflies, we'll get busy again.

Tyler stays here year-round, except for a few weeks in the winter, and then my neighbor helps out with the animals in the barn and any errands I need, like stacking and moving wood or helping with the feed bags. Tyler is in his twenties, full of energy, and with unending strength. All things that are behind me now. I still take care of the house and do some cooking, but find myself sitting more and more in between tasks.

And you, not even forty yet. Having your children young gives you freedom when you're still young enough to enjoy it. I'm sure you're feeling a bit blue with Meg leaving home, but I hope you have some fun planned and embrace your freedom.

I'll be home if you find yourself looking for a place to visit.

Sending love to you,
Jewel

OCTOBER 10, 2022

Dear Micki,

You've been on my mind lately. The beautiful mums you always loved in the deep purples and oranges of fall decorate my porch. Although most are done, I still have a couple of those huge sunflowers you always favored, blooming. They were stunning this year. I always look forward to spring and the bulbs that bring the first bursts of color, and then, of course, my favorite, lavender. I hope I get the chance to see another season.

As the weather turns colder and I'm feeling a bit weaker, memories are my constant companion. Some of my favorites are of the holidays spent with all the kids here at the farm. I'm sure you're looking forward to Meg and Chad being home with you for the holidays.

In your last letter you mentioned Meg being upset with you and not speaking to you. I do hope she's found her way back to you. Over all my years of fostering, I've learned that young women often lash out at their mothers, or the person they look to as a mother. Many times, it's just the young lady spreading her wings and struggling between independence and still longing for the safety and security of her mother.

Have faith, dear heart, that things will get better between the two of you. I know how precious both of your children are to you, and as they mature, there are always rough patches that require careful navigation.

Enjoy the holidays, my dear. My door is always open to you, and if you find the time to visit, I will cherish it.

With love,
Jewel

EPILOGUE

In early January, at eighty-two, Jewel passes away and leaves instructions in her will that impact the lives of all five women.

The next book in the series, *Pathway to Lavender Valley*, features Harriet 'Harry' McKenzie. She is newly retired from her position as Deputy Chief of Investigations at the Salem Police Department and is wondering what to do with the rest of her life.

Her old partner, Tim, passed away less than a month ago, and his loss spurs her to reevaluate her life. As she comes to terms with his death, Harry is prompted to do more than think about retirement. Instead of continuing her career, she's determined to enjoy life and not end up slumped over her desk.

With Tim gone, Harry takes his dog, a sweet golden retriever named Chief, and vows to start a new chapter of her own. She's not quite sure what that will mean, and as she contemplates her new chapter, Jewel's final wish leads her back to Lavender Valley.

You can read Harry's story in PATHWAY TO LAVENDER VALLEY, the next book in the Sisters of the Heart Series.

Six women. Four decades. One long, unexpected reunion.

Book 1: Greetings from Lavender Valley
Book 2: Pathway to Lavender Valley
Book 3: Sanctuary at Lavender Valley
Book 4: Blossoms at Lavender Valley
Book 5: Comfort at Lavender Valley
Book 6: Reunion at Lavender Valley

ACKNOWLEDGMENTS

I've been noodling an idea for a new series for several months before I started writing this one. The idea of foster sisters who never knew each other and are reunited decades later intrigued me. I'm so excited to share the stories of these six women with readers. I love the setting, in the southern part of Oregon and had such fun creating the lives for these women. The series is all filled with furry friends, who are always some of my favorite characters.

My thanks to my editor, Angela, for finding my mistakes and helping me polish *Greetings from Lavender Valley*. She does an awesome job and I'm grateful for her. This gorgeous cover and all the covers in the series are the result of the talents of Elizabeth Mackey, who never disappoints. I'm fortunate to have such an incredible team helping me.

I so appreciate all of the readers who have taken the time to tell their friends about my work and provide reviews of my books. These reviews are especially important in promoting future books, so if you enjoy my novels, please consider leaving a review. I also encourage you to follow me on book retailers, Goodreads, and BookBub, where leaving a review is even easier, and you'll be the first to know about new releases and deals.

Remember to visit my website at http://www.tammylgrace.com and join my mailing list for my exclusive group of readers. I also have a fun Book Buddies Facebook Group. That's the best place to find me and get a chance to participate in my giveaways.

Join my Facebook group at
https://www.facebook.com/groups/AuthorTammyLGraceBookBuddies/
and keep in touch—I'd love to hear from you.

Happy Reading,

Tammy

FROM THE AUTHOR

Thank you for reading GREETINGS FROM LAVENDER VALLEY. I love all the characters in this new SISTERS OF THE HEART SERIES and am excited for readers to get to know all of them. This introduces you to each of the characters and gives you a peek into their lives over the years. Subsequent books will feature each of them as the main character in her own story. The second book, PATHWAY TO LAVENDER VALLEY, will tell Harry's story. She's a character I loved from the first time I thought about her.

If you enjoy women's fiction and haven't yet read the entire HOMETOWN HARBOR SERIES, you can start the series with a free prequel that is in the form of excerpts from Sam's journal. She's the main character in the first book, FINDING HOME.

If you're a new reader and enjoy mysteries, I write a series that features a lovable private detective, Coop, and his faithful golden retriever, Gus. If you like whodunits that will keep you guessing until the end, you'll enjoy the COOPER HARRINGTON DETECTIVE NOVELS.

The two books I've written as Casey Wilson, A DOG'S HOPE and A DOG'S CHANCE have received enthusiastic support from my readers and if you're a dog lover, are must reads.

If you enjoy holiday stories, be sure and check out my CHRISTMAS IN SILVER FALLS SERIES and HOMETOWN CHRISTMAS SERIES. They are small-town Christmas stories of hope, friendship, and family. You won't want to miss any of the SOUL SISTERS AT CEDAR MOUNTAIN LODGE BOOKS, also featuring a foster sister theme. It's a connected Christmas series I wrote with four author friends. My contributions, CHRISTMAS WISHES, CHRISTMAS SURPRISES, and CHRISTMAS SHELTER. All heartwarming, small-town holiday stories that I'm sure you'll enjoy. The series kicks off with a free prequel novella, CHRISTMAS SISTERS, where you'll get a chance to meet the characters during their first Christmas together.

You won't want to miss THE WISHING TREE SERIES, set in Vermont. This series centers on a famed tree in the middle of the quaint town that is thought to grant wishes to those who tie them on her branches. Readers love this series and always comment how they are full of hope, which we all need more of right now.

I'd love to send you my exclusive interview with the canine companions in my Hometown Harbor Series as a thank-you for joining my exclusive group of readers. You can sign up www.tammylgrace.com by clicking this link: https://wp.me/P9umIy-e

ALSO BY TAMMY L. GRACE

COOPER HARRINGTON DETECTIVE NOVELS
Killer Music
Deadly Connection
Dead Wrong
Cold Killer

HOMETOWN HARBOR SERIES
Hometown Harbor: The Beginning (Prequel Novella)
Finding Home
Home Blooms
A Promise of Home
Pieces of Home
Finally Home
Forever Home
Follow Me Home

CHRISTMAS STORIES
A Season for Hope: Christmas in Silver Falls Book 1
The Magic of the Season: Christmas in Silver Falls Book 2
Christmas in Snow Valley: A Hometown Christmas Book 1
One Unforgettable Christmas: A Hometown Christmas Book 2
Christmas Wishes: Souls Sisters at Cedar Mountain Lodge
Christmas Surprises: Soul Sisters at Cedar Mountain Lodge

GLASS BEACH COTTAGE SERIES

Beach Haven

Moonlight Beach

Beach Dreams

WRITING AS CASEY WILSON

A Dog's Hope

A Dog's Chance

WISHING TREE SERIES

The Wishing Tree

Wish Again

Overdue Wishes

SISTERS OF THE HEART SERIES

Greetings from Lavender Valley

Pathway to Lavender Valley

Sanctuary at Lavender Valley

Remember to subscribe to Tammy's exclusive group of readers for your gift, only available to readers on her mailing list. **Sign up at www.tammylgrace.com. Follow this link to subscribe at https://wp.me/P9umIy-e** and you'll receive the exclusive interview she did with all the canine characters in her Hometown Harbor Series.

Follow Tammy on Facebook by liking her page. You may also follow Tammy on book retailers or at BookBub by clicking on the follow button.

ABOUT THE AUTHOR

Tammy L. Grace is the *USA Today* bestselling and award-winning author of the Cooper Harrington Detective Novels, the bestselling Hometown Harbor Series, and the Glass Beach Cottage Series, along with several sweet Christmas novellas. Tammy also writes under the pen name of Casey Wilson for Bookouture and Grand Central. You'll find Tammy online at www.tammylgrace.com where you can join her mailing list and be part of her exclusive group of readers. Connect with Tammy on Facebook at www.facebook.com/tammylgrace.books or Instagram at @authortammylgrace.

- facebook.com/tammylgrace.books
- twitter.com/TammyLGrace
- instagram.com/authortammylgrace
- bookbub.com/authors/tammy-l-grace
- goodreads.com/tammylgrace

Made in United States
Cleveland, OH
02 May 2025